This book belongs to:

This book is for the girl who can't see that she's beautiful. This book is for those who struggle with things that others find easy. This book is for the boy who's just like his friends on the inside, if only they could learn to see beyond the outside. This book is for the ones who doubt themselves and their exquisite strength. This book is for the one who needs a hand and for the hand that grabs hold. This book is for you.

~ AZ

To my boys, Luca and Leo - you are the lights of my life. I am in awe of you both and always inspired. I love you when you're mad, sad, smiling, crying, listening, or not listening. I love each and every part of you. To my family and friends, I'm the luckiest woman alive to have you and your unwavering support. Mom, you are my solid rock.

To my insanely talented illustrator and patient partner in crime, Bill. Thank you for getting me even when I don't get myself and for believing in and loving our Bernadette. You're the peanut butter to my jelly.

To all of you who believed in this little bird and in me, you are my forever family. And finally, to our sweet, sweet Bernadette. I set out to save you, but you turned around and saved me. Thank you for choosing me, and thank you for teaching so many of us the real meaning of bravery and beauty. Your mark is permanent and so far reaching.

Always stand tall, sweet girl.

~ BM

To a little bird who brought so many together.

Bernadette the Brave
By Allison Zapata
Illustrated by Bill Megenhardt

Illustrations are watercolor and colored pencil.
Book design and layout by Bill Megenhardt.

SUMMARY: A little bird, Bernadette, has problems dealing with independent living because of a physical challenge. A bond is created with a small boy when he helps her get healthy through kindness.

ISBN: 978-0-9913761-2-4
Library of Congress registration number 2016937014

Printed in CANADA

Published by Brave Friend Publishing
Houston, Texas

For more information about this book:
bernadettethebrave@gmail.com

For more information about the author:
www.allisonzapata.com

For more information about the illustrator:
megenhardtstudio@yahoo.com

Bernadette the BRAVE

Written by **Allison Zapata**

Illustrated by **Bill Megenhardt**

The trees were working overtime to
welcome back their leaves,
while sparrows were busy building
homes in tiny nooks and eaves.
Flowers were finally waking
from a long winter's nap,
as the woodpeckers played their favorite song -
tap, tap, tap.
The sunny skies and small bird cries could
only mean one thing -
the time had come to bid winter farewell
and wave hello to spring.

Early one morning atop
a tall oak tree,
a cardinal felt her tiny
babies fighting to break free.
The first egg hatched,
then three more,
and just like that
she was a mama to four.

In the beginning
things were normal,
and nothing was the matter.
She kept her babies warm and clean
and fed them when they chattered.
Just two weeks later, the time had
come to send them on their way.
She said goodbye one by one,
and watched them fly away.

All four fledglings
ventured out,
anxious to explore.

They searched for food
and stopped to play.
They spread their wings
and soared.

That evening she watched her brothers finish dinner, all full and feeling well.

But this little girl wasn't so lucky, and had yet to crack a shell.

It felt impossible no matter how hard she tried,

so with nothing else left to do, she perched on a branch and cried.

Up until then everything seemed fine, and she didn't think herself unique.

But later that night, as she fell asleep hungry, she knew her future was bleak.

Early the next morning
she was awoken by the sun
and her tummy's great big rumble.
She wiped the sleep away from her eyes,
then off to the birdbath she stumbled.

Two others had beaten her there:
a pigeon and a grackle.
One of them yelled,
"What's wrong with your face?"
and they both let out a cackle.

"You look so strange,
different than anyone I've seen."
the other one chimed in, being just as mean.

Scared and confused, she lowered her head to find her reflection staring back.
The bottom of her beak was long and scraggly, and down the middle ran a crack.

The top of her beak was even worse -
it was nothing much more than a sliver.
As she thought to herself, "I'm in serious trouble,"
her body began to shiver.

The days crept by slowly,
but quickly turned into weeks.
She got by on fallen seeds from other birds' beaks.
Over time she grew weaker and felt her energy fade.
It was much too hard to walk or fly,
so she spent most days in the shade.

Her beautiful plumage had lost most of its color, once a vibrant tangerine.

And little by little her feathers fell out, until she had nothing left to preen.

Ashamed of the way she looked, she kept her head hung low.

And just when she thought things couldn't get worse, her beak continued to grow.

Comfort came only in dreams,
when she had friends
and the perfect face.
But sure enough,
when she opened her eyes,
she was still the same disgrace.

That morning started out normal, just like any other day.

Little did this bird know how much luck was headed her way.

As she sat quietly in the shade to escape the heat,

out of the corner of her eye appeared a small pair of feet.

"Hi there pretty birdie, why do you look so sad?"
Startled, she glanced up to see a curious looking lad.

She spun around to see
who this pretty bird could be.
She looked up and down, left and right,
and then up in the tree.

"Funny girl, I'm talking to you!"
the boy said with a grin.
"Now come on over and have a bite?
You're looking awfully thin."

She gave it a go and tried cracking the shell like a hundred times before.
But one hundred and one was exactly the same - it fell uneaten to the floor.

"Wait, you can't eat that, huh?
Now I understand."
So he picked them up, one by one,
and cracked them with his hands.
After breaking them into pieces
he tossed her the perfect bite.
She tried once more
and succeeded,
much to their delight.
A second bite followed,
then three, then four,
and she ate and ate until
she could eat no more.

"Come again tomorrow
and I'll bring you something yummy!"
exclaimed the nice boy who had just filled
her tummy.

The next day she jumped when her dinner began to wiggle.

"Those are worms! For you to eat!" her friend said with a giggle.

Over the weeks,
her visits grew longer.
Her color slowly brightened,
and her body became stronger.

Along their journey, he taught her ways that she could help herself,
and make the most out of her life, and this hand that she'd been dealt.

They were unlikely friends, the kind boy and feathered fighter,
who'd somehow learned to trust each other,
and formed a bond that couldn't be tighter.

"You know, I've wanted to name you since the first day we met.
So from now on, if you approve, I'd like to call you Bernadette.

No, wait!

Bernadette the Brave!

Now tell me, sweet friend, what do you say?"
Bernadette answered with a smile,
and felt her sadness slip away.

That joyful moment was soon interrupted
by a blue jay's sudden squawk.
When Bernadette looked up, flying right at her
was a hungry Cooper's Hawk.

The boy threw his body as hard as he could
and, all in one fell swoop,
guarded Bernadette and shouted so loudly
he scared away the Coop.

When peace returned it brought something familiar she'd felt with just one other. Unconditional love and complete acceptance, like that she'd received from her mother.

Over time, B stopped hating herself and feeling so ashamed.

With her head held high, little by little, confidence was claimed.

There were days she felt pretty and thought her beak was kind of cool.

The others also noticed and stopped being so cruel.

She learned to speak up and how to stand her ground.

The name she'd been given indeed fit her well,

for it was bravery that she'd found.

B longed to thank her friend for the kindness he'd bestowed,
and for always sticking by her down a long and difficult road.
She told him with her eyes all the things she had to say.
But did he understand her? She could only hope and pray.

Her question was answered by the sound of his voice fighting to hold back tears.

"What you've given to me, I could never repay—not in a million years."

He thanked Bernadette for the many lessons learned,

and vowed to spend the rest of his life making sure these gifts were returned.

It was then that she knew no words were needed
to communicate her affection,
because deep inside they were exactly the same
and had a natural connection.
Friendship can be found in the most unexpected places.
It comes in all shape and sizes,
reaching across species and races.

With the help of her friend, B learned how to survive.
And by believing in herself, she'd started to thrive.
She realized beauty didn't mean always doing as she was told,
acting like everyone else, or fitting a certain mold.
Because real beauty comes from a different place -
like helping others, loving yourself,
and fighting back with grace.

B taught her friend to open his eyes and see the world as a whole,
instead of closing them to the pain of others just because it hurt his soul.
Through her he had learned all creatures are worthy and deserve a helping hand.
And that it's especially the smallest, those without a voice,
who need someone to take a stand.

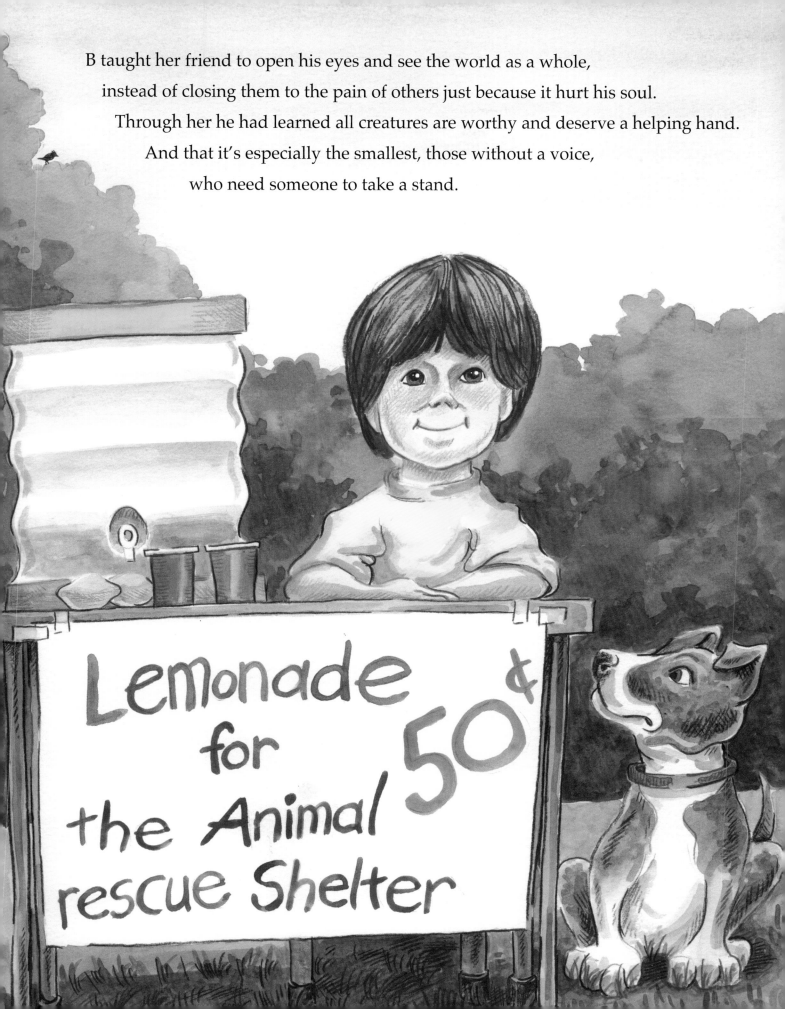

Lemonade
for
the Animal
rescue Shelter
50¢

With the sun shining on her and luck by her side, everything was finally clear.

What challenged her the very most was the reason she was here.

She no longer felt cheated or wished for a different fate,

because she knew what she'd been sent for, and that her purpose was great.

She was chosen for this mission, above all the rest.

Could others accept B for who she was?

This was their test.

That evening while perched at the top of a tree,
the same one where life had started,
B thought about how happy she was -
no longer broken-hearted.
When she asked herself what more she needed,
she could think of only one thing.
And right at that moment, a few branches over,
a red cardinal began to sing.

The Story of Allison and Bernadette

You can call it fate, dumb luck, or divine intervention, but something brought these two together to tell their story. Allison, an avid feeder of birds in her backyard, noticed a unique female cardinal among the bunch. It didn't take long for Allison to realize that, despite her persistence and determination, this bird wasn't able to eat on her own like the others. With equal determination, Allison began experimenting with various meal combinations in hopes it would help this sickly bird survive. Eventually, Allison gave her the name Bernadette, which means "brave as a bear."

Chronicling her adventures with Bernadette, Allison posted updates to her online readers about Bernadette's condition. Interest in this little bird quickly grew and, in time, these updates became a daily necessity for many. It was obvious to Allison that this story needed to be told because, young or old, it's impossible not to fall in love with the spirit of the tiny bird known as—
Bernadette the Brave.